HÅKON ØVREÅS

BLACK

ILLUSTRATED BY
ØYVIND TORSETER

TRANSLATED FROM NORWEGIAN BY
KARI DICKSON

Enchanted Lion Books
NEW YORK

NORLA
Norwegian
Literature Abroad

This translation has been published
with the financial support of NORLA,
Norwegian Literature Abroad.
Enchanted Lion gratefully acknowledges
this support.

www.enchantedlion.com

First English-language edition, published in 2023 by Enchanted Lion Books
248 Creamer Street, Studio 4, Brooklyn, NY 11231
First published in Norway as *Svartle*
Original Norwegian-language edition copyright © 2015 by Gyldendal Norsk Forlag AS
English-language translation copyright © 2023 by Kari Dickson
All rights reserved under International and Pan-American Copyright Conventions
A CIP is on record with the Library of Congress
ISBN: 978-1-59270-275-6 (hardcover); 978-1-59270-268-8 (trade paper)

Printed in Latvia by Livonia Print
First Printing

MIX
Paper | Supporting
responsible forestry
FSC
www.fsc.org
FSC® C002795

When Jack's father started clearing out the garage,
he gave Jack four bags of empty bottles to recycle and
said Jack could keep the money. It was a Saturday
morning, and as Jack trudged through the underpass to
the shop, he thought about what kind of candy he would
buy. The bags were heavy, and he had to hold on to
one of the handles with his pinkie. To manage, he had
to put the bags down several times before reaching the
shop. His fingers, marked with red splotches and white
ridges from the pressure, looked wounded.

The shopkeeper was outside, bending down over a pile of newspapers and ripping off the plastic wrapper. He was wearing a hoodie, and his hair was long and messy.

"Look at that hen!" he said as he straightened up and noticed Jack coming toward him. "The mayor's finest!"

The shopkeeper's long, static hair was sticking out now in all directions. Jack had no idea what he was talking about. He stopped and put down the bags beside him. The shopkeeper picked up one of the newspapers. There was a picture of the mayor holding a hen on the front page. He was smiling and showing off his gold medal.

"And now he's won a prize, as well!" the shopkeeper almost shouted. "A real prizewinning hen!"

"I've come to recycle these bottles," Jack said. "They must be worth at least some pocket money."

"Imagine having a hen like that," the shopkeeper said. "You'd be rich! Apparently, the prize was worth thousands!"

"Wow," Jack said.

The shopkeeper was starstruck. He looked at the photograph for a long time before putting the papers in the stand.

"Aren't you going to count the bottles?" Jack asked.

"Of course," the shopkeeper said, but right then, a black car pulled up in front of the shop. A woman

The scandals near you

Hulebak Times

Egg-straordinary Winner

There's no need for the mayor to take a feather from anyone else's cap anytime soon. On Friday, he won gold for Most Beautiful Hen at this year's National Exhibition.

"I'm so proud," crowed the egg-static mayor.

Marsh Bird Grocery
Eats & Treats

SALE! SALE! SALE!
Half-price awnings

Went to Work in Underpants
"I slept in and forgot to put on my pants," says Graham (78).

Took Taxi to Sweden to Buy Pizza
"I was very hungry," says Terry (55).

Bacon Makes You Smart
Good news story

in a red dress and high heels got out. She marched inside without so much as a glance at Jack and the shopkeeper. Curiously, the car had dark windows, so Jack couldn't see if there was anyone else inside. But before long, the woman was back outside.

"Doesn't anyone work here?" she snapped.

"I do," the shopkeeper said.

He ran his fingers through his hair in an attempt to tidy it, then disappeared into the shop behind her.

Jack tried to pick up the bags, but the handles on one were now ripped. The bottles spilled out, rolling across the sidewalk, as well as under the car. Jack dashed around picking them up, tossing them back into the bag one by one. To get the bottle that had rolled under the car, he lay down on his stomach.

When he stood up again, the car window was open. Inside was a girl, looking right at him. Jack was so surprised, he jumped back, tripping over another bag of empty bottles. More bottles rolled out. He looked at the girl. She was chomping on gum and looked at him with angry eyes. Jack thought her long, black hair glittered. He straightened up. He felt his cheeks flush, and his heart started beating faster, too.

"What are you doing under our car?" the girl asked.

Jack cleared his throat; his mouth was dry, and his voice failed him.

"Can't you speak?" the girl asked, rolling her eyes.

"Bottles," Jack said in a reedy voice that was almost inaudible.

The girl blew an enormous bubble.

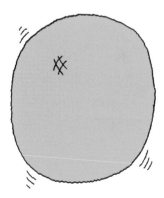

Jack stood and watched the bubble expand until it burst and stuck to her lips.

"Do you have to stare at me like that?" the girl asked.

Jack scurried after the bottles on the ground. He heard the girl blow another bubble, which also burst. When he had gathered up all the bottles, he straightened up again.

"I'll get a lot of money for these," Jack said.

The girl snorted. Then the woman came back out of the shop. She swung a full bag of food onto the back seat and got in. The girl's window slid slowly up, and her face disappeared behind the dark glass. All Jack could see was a reflection of his own face. Then, the car sped off.

The shopkeeper came back out. His hair looked messy again.

EATS
TREATS

Bright and early the next morning, Jack's mother called upstairs to say that Lou was at the door. Jack was still in bed, so he had to throw on some clothes. As he climbed down the ladder from his loft room, he stopped to rub his eyes and nearly fell down the rungs. Lou was sitting in the kitchen waiting for him, and when she saw how sleepy he was, she laughed with her mouth open so wide that Jack could count how many teeth she'd lost. Jack's mom had made her a cup of hot chocolate.

"I want hot chocolate, too," Jack said.

"You don't have time," Lou said. "Some new people have moved into the old bakery!"

"You have to eat something before you go out," his mom said.

Suddenly, there was strange crackling noise from under the table. Lou pulled out a bag. There were now small beeps coming from it.

"Ooooh, they're so noisy," Lou said.

She took out two walkie-talkies and started to twiddle one of the knobs.

"When did you get walkie-talkies?" Jack asked.

"I got them from my sister," Lou said. "But they're total junk. They'll give us away if they keep beeping like that."

"Can I try?" Jack said.

"Maybe later," Lou said. "We have to get Rusty and make a plan."

"I'll just have something to eat first," Jack said.

"But we don't have time. We have spying to do."

Jack and Lou stood in front of Rusty's open front door. Jack had a slice of bread in his hand, and Lou couldn't keep still. Rusty was tying the laces on his sneakers when his dad stuck his head out into the hall.

"It's not like we can fly, Dad," said Rusty. "I mean, it's not like we're superheroes, or anything…"

Jack and Lou stifled their laughter, and Rusty's father raised an eyebrow.

"We're going spying," Lou said, showing him the walkie-talkies. They weren't beeping any longer.

"That sounds exciting," Rusty's dad said. "I know exactly what you need then!"

He disappeared without a word, but was soon back, with a pair of binoculars. He hung them around Rusty's neck.

"It's almost impossible to spy without binoculars," he said.

"Thank you," Lou said.

Rusty's father bowed and went back inside.

"I've got about twenty binoculars at home," Jack told Lou. "My uncle used to work in a binocular shop."

"Then maybe we should get a pair for each of us," Lou said.

"No, we can't," Jack said. "They're so rare that they can't be used."

"Who are we going to spy on?" Rusty asked.

"That's what we're going to find out," Lou said.

The path through the forest was scattered with yellow leaves. They headed toward the old bakery. Jack had picked up a long branch and was pretending to fence. Rusty looked through the binoculars as he walked.

"Mom said there was a moving van in front of the bakery," Lou said. "And there was a piano inside."

"Why would you want a piano in a bakery?" Jack asked.

"A family's moving into the bakery, silly," Lou said. "They're making it into a home."

"But there's nothing weird about that," Rusty said.

"You're right, but I'm going to be a private detective when I grow up," Lou said. "So, I need to practice spying. And for that, you need someone you don't know."

"My granddad was a spy during the war," Jack said. "He was taken prisoner by the enemy and had to escape through a sewage pipe."

"Yuck," Lou said. "I definitely don't want to do that kind of spying."

When they reached the slope by the bakery, they hung back among the trees. The old building looked like an enormous Lego block. Lou broke off a spruce branch and stuck it in Rusty's hair.

"What are you doing?" he asked.

"We can't risk being seen," Lou said, sticking another twig down his T-shirt.

"That's scratchy," Rusty said.

"We can't be cowards now," Lou said. "Do you think Jack's grandfather would have complained if it was scratchy?"

She smiled at Jack, and Jack stuck a big branch down the back of his T-shirt so that it fanned over him like a big umbrella.

"Okay, it's only a little scratchy," Rusty said.

They lay down at the top of the slope by the bakery. The ground was wet, and Jack felt the damp seep into his knees and arms. But it was nearly impossible to spot them. It was almost as if three new bushes had sprung up in a matter of minutes, with a pair of binoculars

sticking out of one of them. Rusty was the first to use the binoculars. The door to the bakery was closed.

"Can you see them?" Lou asked, tugging at the strap of the binoculars.

"It doesn't look very nice inside," Rusty said. "All I can see are cardboard boxes."

"I bet thieves live there," Jack said. "I've heard that they don't live in nice houses, in case they end up going to jail. That way, they won't miss home as much."

"That's the dumbest thing I've ever heard," Lou said. "Everyone wants to have a nice home."

"Maybe they're vampires," Rusty said.

"Vampires?" Lou laughed. "That's even dumber than thieves."

"Well, if they're vampires, they don't need to have a nice place," Rusty said. "They'd be up most of the night and only care about blood."

"A vampire family?" Lou said. "That's like those stupid movies my sister watches. I couldn't care less about them."

"Well, we can't be sure that they're not vampires," Rusty said.

"If they're vampires, I have better things to do than spy on them for long," Lou said. "Vampires are really childish."

It was Jack's turn to look through the binoculars. The factory windows were big and dark. Some were covered with brown paper on the inside. He thought he saw a small, flickering flame in one window, a candle, but he couldn't be sure. He spied a tower of cardboard boxes through another window.

"Maybe we should find out if they're vampires," Lou said. "Then we can warn the town council."

Jack turned the binoculars around and looked through the big end. The old bakery was now tiny, and it looked far, far away. All was quiet by the edge of the forest, and dark clouds trudged across the sky. The treetops had started to sway in the wind. Suddenly, they heard a creaking sound coming from the bakery.

"Look!" Jack shouted.

He pointed at the garage as he quickly turned the binoculars back the right way. The garage door had slowly started to open.

"Shhh," Lou whispered. "Don't give us away."

When the door was completely up, a black car with dark windows emerged. As soon as the car drove off, the garage door started to close.

"That's a very mysterious car," Rusty said.

"I don't think they saw us," Lou said.

"Maybe they're spies, since they have such a mysterious car," Rusty said.

"But we're the spies," Jack said. "What would they spy on?"

"Maybe they're spying on the town council," Lou said. "My mom works at the council, and they have lots of secrets in the basement."

"If they're spies, we'll have to call the police," Rusty said.

"When my grandfather was a spy, he stole all the

enemy's maps," Jack said. "He did it so the enemy would get lost and end up in the mountains. And once, he stole a whole lot of dynamite from the enemy that he gave to the good guys."

"That's wild," Lou said.

Jack could feel light rain on his face. It had started to drizzle. He handed the binoculars back to Rusty. While Rusty studied the dark windows, it started coming down harder. Jack shivered and stood up.

"What are you doing?" Lou cried. "You can't stand up!"

"But they're gone," Jack said.

"You just can't," Lou said. "There might still be someone inside. We should go and investigate around the back."

She got up into a crouch. Rusty did the same. Jack could feel that he was wet, and the spruce branch down the back of his T-shirt was itching more and more.

"I'll stay here and keep guard," he said. "In case they escape."

"The two of us can go," Rusty said to Lou.

Lou took the walkie-talkies out of the bag. She gave one to Jack.

"Press this button if you want to say anything," she said.

Jack lay back down at the top of the slope, while Lou and Rusty ran around to the back of the building. The branch was rubbing against his skin. He managed to get rid of a few twigs, but the big branch was stuck in the fabric of his T-shirt. Jack stood up and tugged at the branch. It scraped his back. There was a loud crackling from the walkie-talkie. He quickly pressed the button that Lou had shown him, but nothing happened. The crackling hurt his ears. He pressed all the buttons he could find. The worst of the static died down, but there was still a faint beeping. Then suddenly, it was quiet again. Jack looked around for Lou and Rusty. But all he saw was a girl standing outside the bakery.

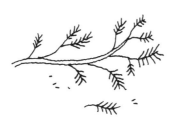

Jack jumped. *Where had she sprung from?* He froze and didn't dare to look at her. Instead, he hid behind the needles on his branch. Maybe it was a vampire girl.

Jack stayed totally still. He was too shocked to move even a finger.

"You don't need to pretend to be a tree," said the girl. "I've already seen you!"

Jack moved his arm cautiously.

"Spying is really childish," she said.

He looked at her. Then, he realized who it was. It was the girl from the car outside the shop. His heart did a somersault in his chest. He cleared his throat.

"Um … we just wanted to make sure you weren't dead," Jack said.

"Dead?"

"Yes, as in not alive."

"Why wouldn't we be alive?"

"Or you might come alive at night. You might be the type of person who doesn't like daylight," Jack muttered.

The girl laughed out loud.

"You thought I was a vampire! Haha!"

"Of course not," Jack said. "I was only joking."

The girl laughed even more.

"Isn't spying on vampires dangerous?"

"Well, are you one?" Jack asked.

The girl couldn't stop laughing.

"There are actually vampires in the United States," Jack said. "A friend of my dad's had to fight off three of them once, in a fancy steakhouse. Luckily, he discovered they were allergic to ketchup."

The girl was laughing so hard now that she doubled over, and Jack started to laugh, too. He finally managed to pull the branch out from his T-shirt.

The walkie-talkie beeped again, and behind all the crackling, he could hear Lou's voice.

"Rusty and Lou to Jack," she said. "We've been around the whole building, no sign of life, but there's some really weird furniture. Over!"

Jack pressed all the buttons to turn it off. When he looked up from the walkie-talkie, the girl was serious again.

"In any case, you can't spy," the girl said. "It's really childish. And illegal."

She turned and went back into the bakery. The door clicked shut behind her, and Jack was left standing there.

Not long after, Rusty and Lou appeared like two walking bushes.

"Weren't you going to keep watch?" Lou said. She looked at the spruce branch and twigs lying all around Jack.

"There's lots of garbage back there," Rusty said. "It's not easy to see anything at all."

"They've got an old dentist's chair!" Lou said. "Rusty saw it."

"Could we do something else?" Jack said. "Maybe we could build some more of the hut, for example?"

"You were supposed to keep watch," Lou repeated.

"Anyway, I think it's illegal to spy on people," Jack said, giving the walkie-talkie back to Lou. "Maybe we should quit while we're ahead."

Rusty and Lou pulled out their branches, too, and they all headed back to the edge of the forest. Jack turned around to see if he could catch a glimpse of the girl, but the windows were as dark as before.

"It would be best if we could watch the house night and day," Lou said. "Then they wouldn't be able to get away so easily."

Jack didn't say anything. The sun came out and shone through the trees, lighting up the path in front of them. The wet leaves glistened, and Jack tried to jump over the puddles on the path.

That evening, Jack lay in his bed and couldn't sleep. He stared at the ceiling. The room was dark, save for three thin strips of light from the streetlamps outside. He could hear the house creaking, and he thought he heard the new girl laugh. He sat bolt upright in bed. Then he went over to the window. He could see the dark church spire rising over the rooftops, silhouetted against the sky. Past all of the houses, where the forest began, was the old bakery. *It's not possible to hear her laugh from this far away*, Jack thought, noticing how warm he felt.

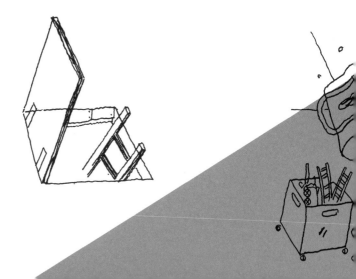

Jack's dad had something strange on his head when he crossed the yard. It looked like a big pile of cardboard. Jack and his mom watched him from the doorway before he disappeared into the garage.

"Who knows what he does in there?" Jack's mom said.

"What are you doing?" Jack called to his dad.

His father just waved back at the two of them.

"It would be better if he finished your new room!" Jack's mom said, and she went back into the house.

Jack put on his shoes and ran outside. His dad was in the middle of the garage. He'd tidied it up, and all his guitars were hanging on the wall. Jack also saw an old green sofa, a brown organ, and amplifiers on the floor. His dad was nailing big egg trays made of cardboard to all of the empty walls. Jack had seen egg trays like these before in the shop.

"Are you going to put eggs on the wall?" Jack asked.

"Looks good, doesn't it?" his father managed to say, despite the nails he held between his teeth. "But no, I'm not going to put eggs in them; it's to mute the sound when I'm playing."

"That's possible?" Jack asked.

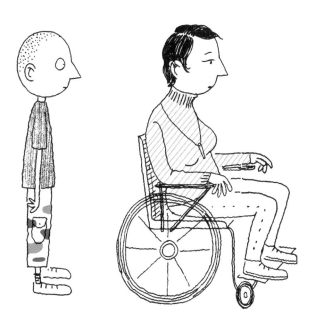

"I got all of this from the mayor," his father said. "He keeps hens and collects their eggs. Did you see the picture of his prizewinning hen in the paper?"

Jack nodded.

"I went to visit Granny," said his dad. "The mayor's right next door."

"Does Granny like hens?" Jack asked.

"I doubt it," his dad laughed.

He started to hammer in another nail. Jack looked around. His dad had pinned up a poster on the wall beside the guitars. Jack had seen it before. It was of his dad and three other men, all with very long hair. The poster was from the old days, when his dad played in a band. It said: "The Angry Cucumbers." That was the name of the band. Jack had to laugh every time he saw that dumb name.

"Why don't you play in a band anymore?"

"I'm going to start again," his dad said. "When the boys get back from the United States, we're going to play again, and we're going to be big. We might even be world-famous. That would be cool, wouldn't it?"

THE ANGRY CUCUMBERS

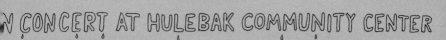

N CONCERT AT HULEBAK COMMUNITY CENTER

Jack nodded.

"It would be really cool," his dad said again. "We'll make lots of money, and we'll travel around the world. To Egypt, India, Japan—all kinds of places. You can come, too!"

"Will it be long until then?" Jack asked.

"It'll be soon, when the boys get back from the U.S."

"But you can't be called 'The Angry Cucumbers,'" Jack said. "That'll sound really stupid everywhere else."

His father laughed and hammered in another nail.

Later, down by the shop, the shopkeeper's van was parked with its doors wide open. When Jack walked past, the shopkeeper came out with boxes full of food that he put into the back of the van. Jack had seen the van outside his granny's house, making a delivery. The shopkeeper lifted a couple of fingers in greeting before slamming the doors shut and driving off, leaving behind a trail of gray exhaust.

Jack was on his way to find Rusty and Lou, but the moment he passed the shop, he went in the other direction. Without thinking, he headed to the forest instead. And suddenly, he was on the path that led to the old bakery.

He hadn't thought of spying again. But here he was. He walked along the top of the slope and peered down at the windows. The brown paper had been removed from two of them and replaced by curtains, and a long shelf of cactuses stretched across both windows. Jack slowed down. As he passed the bakery, he realized that he would need to go in the opposite direction to get back into town. So he turned around and walked past the bakery again. He thought a boy should be allowed to go for a walk in the forest without it being childish, especially if he wasn't spying. When he passed the bakery again, he pretended to be looking up at the treetops. He kept walking back and forth through the trees in front of the bakery until the door eventually opened. It was the girl. She came out and put her hands on her hips.

"Are you spying on me again?" she said.

"No, I was just walking past," Jack said.

"Like a hundred times?" the girl said.

"Oh, there are some very rare birds here," Jack said. "You won't believe your eyes when you see them."

"Oh, really?" said the girl, without looking up at the trees.

"A professor once came all the way from Russia to see the rare birds," Jack said. "But I think they've flown away now; you must have scared them."

"I still think you're spying," the girl said.

"I've stopped doing that," Jack said. "It was really childish."

"And illegal," the girl said.

"But a walk in the forest is allowed," Jack retorted quickly.

"Show me your stupid birds," the girl said, "if you're really not still spying on me."

Jack turned around and looked up at the trees. It felt like he had an enormous stone in his stomach. The girl looked up at the trees, too.

"Just as I thought…" she started to say.

But she was interrupted by some strange sounds. They both craned their necks. The strange trumpet sounds were coming from the forest. Then they saw three big birds rising up into the sky. They had long necks, and their huge wings clipped the tops of the trees, right above their heads.

"Wow!" the girl said.

Jack stood there for a long time without saying anything. *How strange!* The birds disappeared over the bakery roof, the trumpet sounds faded, and still, Jack stood there staring up into the sky.

"Wow," the girl said again. "You weren't lying."

"Um … of course not," Jack said. "I never lie."

He went down to the front of the bakery where the girl was standing.

"That was amazing," the girl said, looking up at the treetops where the birds had appeared.

"What's your name?" Jack asked.

The girl glanced at Jack but didn't reply. She shrugged.

"What's it like living in a bakery?" Jack asked.

Again, the girl didn't answer, just walked toward the door. When she was about to go in, she turned and looked at Jack.

"Are you coming, or what?"

There were cardboard boxes everywhere inside, in the middle of the room and stacked up against the white brick walls. The girl picked her way between the boxes, and Jack pulled off his dirty shoes and followed. They came to a room where the boxes were piled up high in a corner among lamps and chairs. On the other side of the room was a black sofa.

"My room's up here," the girl said, pointing to a ladder.

"Oh, you've got a ladder, too?" Jack said.

They climbed up to a small room. There were pictures of rock bands pinned to the wall. All the rockers had long, black hair and looked angry. The girl sat down on the chair by her desk. It was by the window, with a view straight into the forest outside, and onto the slope where Jack, Rusty, and Lou had been spying.

"My dad plays in a rock band," Jack said, pointing at the pictures on the wall. "They're probably Norway's best rock band. They're going to be really big soon."

"That's nothing," the girl said. "My mom's so well-known that she can't even walk down the street in America, because everyone wants her autograph."

"Is she that famous?" Jack said.

"I'm not sure how long we can stay here," the girl said. "It might be better to live abroad; we haven't decided yet."

The girl had a stereo system on her desk. Jack pressed play and rock music blasted out. The room

was suddenly full of drums, bass, guitars, and a woman's voice. The girl started to nod to the music. Jack nodded along a little, too, but it felt a bit weird, so he stopped.

"That's actually my mom singing!" the girl shouted over the music.

"Huh?" Jack said.

"That's my mom singing," the girl repeated.

"Why did you move here if you're not going to stay?" Jack shouted.

The girl shrugged.

"It's kind of cool to live in a bakery," Jack said.

"My mom owns lots of houses," the girl said. "We've got an old palace in Italy that's thousands of years old. We have to decide where we like best. But we can only stay here if we get some famous friends, because otherwise it'll be too boring."

She turned up the volume even more and continued nodding to the rhythm.

"I'm Sandy, by the way," she shouted.

"Is your mom really famous?" Jack asked.

Sandy just nodded, but Jack couldn't tell if she was

nodding yes to him, or if she was just getting into the music.

"My name's Jack," Jack said.

But he wasn't sure if she'd heard him. So later, when he was about to leave and they were standing by the door, he said it again.

"My name's Jack."

"You've already said that," Sandy said.

"Maybe I'll see you tomorrow," Jack said, and he started to walk towards the forest.

"We might not be here!" Sandy shouted after him. "I might have to go to Australia with Mom."

As Jack walked along the path home, his ears were still ringing, and he thought he could still feel the beat thumping in his belly.

Jack opened the door to the garage. It was dark inside. He turned on the light and went over to the guitars and egg trays that his dad had hung up. He picked up the guitar that was standing against a chair and sat down. He plucked the strings, and the instrument let out a soft moan. It didn't sound as heavy as the music Sandy had played. He tried again, but he could only get hollow sounds out of the strings. Jack sighed.

"Have you started playing the guitar?" he heard his dad say. He was standing in the doorway, smiling. Jack shrugged.

"I can teach you," his father said.

He came over to Jack and turned a knob, and the amplifier came on. The guitar screeched, making a whole lot of noise. His dad turned down the volume. He moved Jack's fingers and pointed.

"Like this," he said. "You have to do this."

Jack tried to move his fingers in the way his dad had shown him, but it sounded just as bad as before, only louder. No matter how hard he tried, he couldn't make the guitar sound cool.

"Press down harder on the strings," his dad said. "That's it, good."

A few random notes rang out. Jack stopped playing.

"How do you become famous?" Jack asked.

His dad was staring at Jack's fingers.

"You can't stop pressing hard," his dad said. "I'll show you."

He took the guitar from Jack and put it over his

knee. He started to play, and now the guitar sounded happy. Jack sighed to himself; he'd never be any good at playing.

"Do you know how to become famous?" Jack asked again.

"Famous?" his dad said. "Oh, it's not all about being famous. The most important thing is to live for your music!"

He started to play faster, rocking back and forth.

"This is how you should play!" he shouted over the sound, nodding his head.

"Will it make me famous?" Jack asked.

His dad closed his eyes and got lost in a long guitar solo, which he finished with some loud twangs and muted plucks.

"The most important thing is to have fun when you're playing," his father said. "And then, you make a bit of a show of it, like the boys and I did when we played. We could have been really famous if we had wanted."

"Didn't you want to be?" Jack asked.

"We once played a gig, and the crown prince was there," his father said. "He came to see us afterward and said we were really good. He wanted us to go to his country house to play for the king."

"Did you play for the king?"

"Nah, we didn't feel like it," his dad said. "And in any case, we'd already bought our train tickets home."

"You could have been super famous if you'd played for the king!" Jack said.

"Well…" his dad said. "When the boys come back, maybe we'll call the crown prince."

"But that's a long way off," Jack said. "Can I learn to play and be famous, too?"

"Of course you can learn," his dad said. "Watch."

He started to play again, strumming the strings with a quiet tune.

"You can play like this," he said.

Then, he turned the knob on the amplifier, and the sound got even louder than before.

"Or you can play like this," his dad shouted, starting to play faster. "Maybe this is how you get famous!"

He kept on playing. Jack watched his dad's fingers, but couldn't figure out what he was doing. They were running up, down, and across the strings. His dad closed his eyes again and swayed to the rhythm.

Jack kept expecting to get the guitar back so he could try. He got up and stood there, but his dad didn't even notice him. He was so into the music that he didn't see that Jack was waiting, so after a little, Jack just left.

The clouds had gathered overhead, but here and there, the sun still shone through. *Like spotlights on a stage*, Jack thought. He could still hear his father wailing away in the garage. He sighed and went into the house.

The hut that Jack, Lou, and Rusty had built was on a small hill by the edge of the forest, at the back of Lou's house. They'd finished it over the summer. It was so solid that even the bullies couldn't pull it down. The door had a padlock, and there were piles of comics safely inside. Lou, Rusty, and Jack had each painted a wall: blue, brown, and black. And on the fourth wall, Lou had stuck up a whole bunch of pony pictures because she couldn't bear having them in her bedroom anymore. Lou was fiddling with the walkie-talkies, which made faint beeps every now and then. Jack was reading a comic. It was about a superhero who hid his identity by working as a newspaper reporter.

"The best thing would be if we could spy on them all the time," Rusty said. "Then they couldn't get away."

"But we can't be awake all the time," Lou said. "So we'll have to spy in shifts."

"If we're going to spy in shifts, we really need a tent," Rusty said.

"Good idea!" Lou said. "We could use a camouflage tent, like the ones they've got in the army."

Jack looked up from his comic.

"My cousin probably has about twenty army tents," he said, immediately regretting it.

"Oh, could you borrow one?" Lou asked.

"Maybe," Jack said. "Or…I don't know…"

"That would be perfect," Lou said.

"I could ask…" Jack said. "But then again, I don't know if it's so smart to spy on them at all."

"When we get a tent, we can spend the night there as well," Lou said.

"And then we'll be invisible," Rusty said.

"Well, I'm not going to spy," Jack said. He put down the comic. "There's no point anymore."

Rusty and Lou were silent. Lou looked at Rusty, but he shook his head.

"Are you scared of vampires?" Lou asked.

"No," Jack said. "She's not a vampire."

"Who's she?" Lou said.

"They're not vampires," Jack corrected himself.

"Have you spoken to them?" Rusty asked.

"One of them, maybe," Jack said. "She's called Sandy."

"Why did you do that?" Lou asked.

"She just appeared," Jack said.

"Maybe she's actually a ghost?" Rusty suggested.

"No, no, it was just a normal girl who appeared."

"You've ruined everything," Lou said.

"Was she nice?" Rusty asked.

"Probably not," Lou said.

"Her mom's actually really famous," Jack said. "She's a rock star."

"Wow," Rusty said.

"There's nothing special about that," Lou said. "There are lots of rock stars, and most of them are show-offs."

"I heard her music," Jack said.

"Cool," Rusty said. "You heard her mom sing?"

"Just a recording," Jack said.

"I'm going to get my sister's record player," Lou said. "She has lots of good music that I can borrow."

"And Sandy has to climb up a ladder to get to her room," Jack said.

"Just like you!" Rusty said.

Lou stood up and stomped across the floor.

"That's enough!" she shouted. "We were going to have a spy meeting."

"But that's what we're doing," Rusty said. "Jack's got lots of really useful information."

"No," Lou said. "It's not useful. He's ruined everything!"

Lou ran from the hut, slamming the door behind her. Jack and Rusty sat in silence and waited for her to come back. Jack picked up the comic again. He turned the pages, but didn't read.

"I guess I've ruined everything," Jack said after a while.

"I can think of a lot that's not ruined," Rusty said. "Our hut, for example."

Later that day, Jack walked to his granny's house with his dad. It stood on a small hill, and they had to pass the mayor's farm to get there. A big, black dog was out on the step, and it barked and started to bound over to them. But the dog was chained, so it jerked to a stop. Jack's dad laughed as the dog continued to growl. It bared its sharp teeth.

"Take it easy, buddy," he said to the dog. "No need to get so wound up."

Jack skirted around the yard. He passed a chicken run. The hens were so busy pecking the ground that they didn't even look up.

"You weren't frightened of that scrappy dog, were you?" his dad laughed.

"Of course not," Jack said. "I just wanted to see the hens."

"Ah, yes, the prizewinning hen," his dad said, pointing.

A snow-white hen was strutting around among the flock. Her feathers gleamed.

"Imagine, winning first prize!" Jack's dad said.

"Is the mayor very famous?" Jack asked.

The hen cocked her head and looked at Jack. His father kept walking. Jack ran to catch up. The dog continued to bark until they were some way up the road. Jack's granny's house was old and detached, and stood like a castle on the hill. The windows were dark, and some shingles on one side of the roof had started to fall off. Jack stopped when his dad went up the front steps. The doorbell was a lion's head that rang when the tongue was pressed. A huge spider's web hung over the steps.

"I'll just wait down here," Jack said.

75

The door creaked, and his father disappeared inside. Jack stood by the step and looked up at the spider that was climbing around its web in the corner.

"Are you coming?" his father called from inside.

"In a minute," Jack said.

He backed away from the steps. There was a small shed on the far side of the house that looked as if it were leaning its roof against the birch tree, which waved its small, yellow leaves. The rooster down on the mayor's farm crowed twice. Jack waded through the tall, wet grass at the side of the road. He managed to get as far as the hen enclosure without the dog noticing him.

"You're lucky to be so famous," Jack said to the hen. The hen cocked her head, while the other hens picked and pecked around her.

"If we were friends, maybe I'd be famous, too!"

Right then, the dog got wind of Jack. It pulled on its chain and started to bark furiously.

"Take it easy," Jack shouted, "I'm not going to steal your stupid hen!"

Suddenly, Jack froze.

Then, he looked at the dog. He looked at the mayor's house. He looked around the yard, and at the bushes behind the henhouse and the forest beyond.

Jack whispered to himself, "But if some thieves were to steal the hen, then I could rescue it! And then, I'd definitely be in the newspaper."

When his dad came out of his grandmother's house, he stopped and looked around. He called for Jack. Jack came out of the shed at the far side of the house.

"What happened to you?" his dad asked.

"I just wanted to have a look in the old shed," he said.

His father laughed.

"That old pile of wood. It should have been burnt down ages ago."

They set off for home, and as they passed through the mayor's yard, Jack glanced over at the prizewinning hen, as though they had a secret agreement. But the hen was walking around happily, none the wiser.

When they got back, Jack ran up to his room. He lay down on the floor and pulled out an old, blue bag from under the bed. He'd hidden a bundle of clothes in it that he didn't want his mom or dad to find: his superhero clothes. Black. It had been a while now since he, Rusty, and Lou had been superheroes. Not since that night when they had run through the pitch darkness as Black, Brown, and Blue, and had painted those bullies' bikes. They'd almost been caught by the police, but then, the bullies got the blame instead. It made Jack giggle to think about it. He ran his hand over his cape, which he'd made from an old, black jacket that his mother no longer wore.

He pushed the bundle back under the bed and climbed down the ladder. He knew there were some old burlap sacks in the cellar. Jack went down into the cold darkness under the house. He dreaded going down there every time, because it was at least ten steps to the light switch, and the small bulb emitted no more than a faint glow. Jack thought he saw something move under the radiator. He jumped back. Behind the empty jam jars and a toolbox, there was a pile of sacks. They were torn and full of holes, so Jack found the best one. He measured the holes and concluded that none were big enough for a hen to escape through.

He found a packet of sunflower seeds in the kitchen cupboard, and he took the padlock from a big chest in the garage. Luckily, the key was in it. He stowed the key all the way under his bed with the superhero costume.

When night fell, Jack put on that costume. Black was ready for action. But this time, without paint and without his friends. He put the sunflower seeds in his pocket and tucked the sack under his arm. Then he tiptoed down the stairs, trying to step right on the edge of each, so they wouldn't creak. Once outside, he saw there was a full moon. The clouds moved slowly across it. The windows in all the houses along the street were

dark. Black ran as fast as he could to the path that led through the underpass and up to the shop on the other side. Before long, he was approaching his granny's house, and the mayor's farm was just below. All the windows in the mayor's house were dark, too. Black was out of breath by the time he reached the trees by the yard. He left the road and ran around the back of the barn, so the dog wouldn't smell him. The henhouse was only a few feet away. Black crept through the wet grass right up to the enclosure and the door to the henhouse. There was a small hook to keep the door closed. He flicked it up and slipped in. He couldn't hear a sound. The hens were asleep. Black opened up the sack, then crept over to the rows of sleeping hens. He came upon the best-looking one—the prizewinning hen, the hen from the newspaper.

One of the other hens clucked. Black froze. But she seemed to have clucked in her sleep. Black readied himself, and in one swoop, he bagged the prizewinning hen. She didn't make a single sound. And closing the sack was easy. But now, he had awoken another hen who started to cluck and fuss, and soon all the hens were awake, flapping and making noise. Their feathers were flying around, and it was almost impossible to see anything in the small henhouse. Black tried to shush them, but it was too late. Because now the rooster had started to crow as well. Black slung the sack over his back and hurried out the door. He fumbled with the hook. The dog had also started to bark, and Black saw the lights go on in the mayor's house. He refastened the hook and ran off. The sack was very heavy, but he managed to keep it on his back, where it bumped against him. He saw a door in the mayor's house open. Black crept into the long grass behind the henhouse.

The prizewinning hen had stuck her head out of one of the holes in the sack and was looking at Black in surprise.

"You have to keep absolutely still," Black whispered to the hen. "Otherwise, I won't be able to rescue you."

"Quiet!" he heard the mayor shout at the dog.

Black held his breath so he wouldn't make a sound. His heart was racing.

The mayor walked across the yard, talking to the
dog all the while.

"No danger here," he said.

The mayor was at the door to the henhouse.

"You'll scare the hens if you bark like that," he said
to the dog. "See, the door is locked, and everything's
fine. It was probably just a badger on its way home."

He went back across the yard to the house, mumbled something to himself or the dog, and went inside.

Black jumped up, swung the sack over his shoulder, and ran as fast as he could up the hill to his grandmother's house. The windows stayed dark as he crept past the house and made his way to the ramshackle shed by the birch tree. He took the sack inside and opened it.

"You can come out now," he said, trying to sound as kind as he could.

The hen flapped her wings and came out of the sack. She hopped around, clucked, and cocked her head, looking at Black with startled eyes.

"You can stay here for a while," he whispered. "Then I can find you, and we'll both be in the papers!"

The hen started to look around, clucking and flapping her wings every now and then. She went here and there, as if she were inspecting the shed.

"Look what I've got for you," Black said, producing the packet of sunflower seeds. "A little snack. Also, if Granny comes out, you have to hide!"

He emptied the seeds onto the uneven floor. The hen peered down at the small pile. Then, she looked back up at Black.

"I'll see you in the morning," Black said. "I'll be back to rescue you."

He closed the door, pulled the padlock out from his pocket, threaded it through the bolt on the door, and snapped it shut. Now, he could relax. But his heart was still pounding under his superhero costume, and his clothes were soaked from lying in the wet grass. There was a wind blowing outside that tugged and pulled at the branches on the old birch tree. Black shivered. He was freezing. He took off his mask as he ran along the dark roads. By the time he got home, his body was shaking so much that he could barely kick off his shoes before he crept inside. He felt dizzy as he climbed the ladder to his room. He took off his wet superhero costume and buried himself under the covers.

Jack was lying on the sofa in the living room. The house was quiet. The sun had just crept over the top of the hill and was shining through the window, filling the living room with a warm, golden light. The morning after the night he'd taken the mayor's hen, he hadn't been able to get out of bed. His father had had to carry him down the steep ladder.

"You look like a ghost!" his mom said, putting a hand on his forehead. "And you're burning up!"

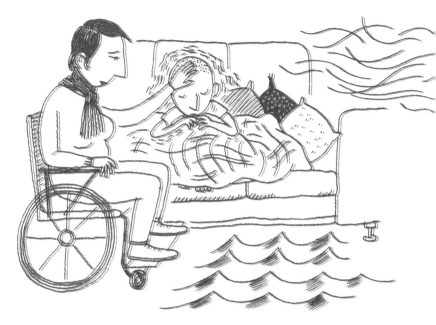

She gave him something to bring down the fever.
But he struggled to swallow it. His body felt floppy,
and everything ached.

"You'll have to stay down here so I can look after
you," his mom said. "You'll be perfectly all right in a
couple of days."

His mother made up a bed on the sofa. Jack went in
and out of sleep. He didn't know whether it was day or
night. Sometimes he sweated; sometimes he shivered,
even though he had two quilts.

He heard the doorbell ring. He heard Rusty's and Lou's voices. His mom told them he wasn't feeling well and that they'd have to come back another day. He heard the door close.

Now, Jack was lying on the sofa in the golden morning light. He no longer felt feverish. In fact, he felt perfectly fine. It was only when he stood up that he felt a little dizzy. No one else was awake. Through the window, he could see the streets were empty. He helped himself to some porridge in the kitchen. Then he pulled on a thick jacket, put on his shoes, and carefully opened the front door. When he got out onto the steps, he realized how cold it was. The sun, which had heated the room, wasn't nearly as warm outside. He zipped up his jacket and set off. He didn't have the energy to run. Even walking tired him out. There was an echo in the underpass on the way to the shop, so Jack normally shouted something whenever he went through it, but now his voice was only a whisper.

As he got closer to his granny's house and the dilapidated shed, he thought he could hear the hen clucking. *Or was it the noise of his footsteps? Or his breathing?* He walked as fast as he could, past the front door and over to the small shed.

Immediately, he saw that the door he had locked with the padlock was open! Rushing in, Jack saw white feathers everywhere, and a few sunflower seeds, but no hen. He searched every inch of the shed. He lifted some rotten planks that were leaning against the wall, but

no hen. There were white feathers outside as well. *Had the hen managed to escape?* Jack inspected the door. The padlock was still closed; someone had broken the bolt itself.

He ran down the hill, past the mayor's house and the angry dog. It was obviously asleep, because it didn't bark. Jack ran all the way to Lou's house, on the outskirts of town. He rang the bell. After a long time, Lou's mother opened the door. She was still in her bathrobe.

"I have to talk to Lou," Jack said.

"But it's six in the morning," her mother said. "Lou's asleep."

"It's a crisis!" Jack said.

Lou's mother told him to come in. She went upstairs, but it wasn't long before she came back down to say that Lou was awake, and he could go up.

"There's a crisis!" he said again as soon as he saw Lou.

She had managed to get dressed but looked like she was still asleep.

"You've got to wake up!" Jack said. "Someone's broken into my granny's shed!"

"Maybe it's those punks again," Lou mumbled.

She meant the boys who had destroyed their hut.

"Maybe," she said, now awake, "they're up to their old tricks."

"I don't know," Jack said. "The lock's been broken, and the hen has vanished!

"What hen?" Lou said, rubbing her eyes.

"Umm ... well, the main thing is that someone has broken in!"

"What kind of hen?" Lou said, narrowing her eyes. "And if someone's broken in, we have to call the police."

"No, we have to find out who the thieves are!" Jack said. "You know a bit about investigation and spying and that kind of thing. There's no time to lose."

They went downstairs, and Lou's mother gave them both breakfast: warm rolls with cheese and hot chocolate. The steam curled up out of the mugs. Jack noticed the newspaper on the table. There was a photograph of the mayor on the front page. He looked angry. "PRIZEWINNING HEN MISSING!" it said in big, black letters.

Jack turned the paper over so Lou wouldn't see the picture. But it was too late.

"Do you think the same people that broke into your granny's shed stole the hen from the mayor?" she asked.

"Maybe," Jack said, hesitantly. "There were a lot of feathers by the shed."

"I see," Lou said. "Then we have a clue. Now we have to find out why the hen thieves broke into the shed."

"You can't be certain that the hen was stolen," Jack said. "Maybe someone just borrowed it and was going to give it back, but then someone else stole it in the meantime."

"No," Lou said. "That's not very likely."

"Maybe someone just wanted to use the hen for a day or two, and then give her back?"

"Why would someone want to borrow a hen?"
Lou asked.

"To get a reward, maybe."

"Kidnap a hen for ransom?" Lou said. "Who would
be that stupid?"

"Well, maybe the person who took the hen wanted
to be in the papers, so that he would be famous?"

"That's ridiculous," said Lou. "We need to think
like real detectives!"

"But what if he got sick in the meantime and wasn't
able to give back the hen? And that's when the thieves
stole it."

Lou put down her cup of hot chocolate. She looked at Jack for a long time.

"He got sick?" she said.

"Yes," Jack said.

He slid as far down in the chair as he could and tried to hide behind what was left of his roll.

"Someone wanted to be in the newspaper and get famous?"

"Yes," Jack said. "Something like that…The most important thing is that we find the thief. And save the hen before she's eaten."

Lou said nothing. She just sat there thinking. Jack drank the rest of his hot chocolate and looked down at the dark, syrupy remains at the bottom of the mug.

"And anyway, it's illegal to break into Granny's shed!" Jack said. "The thief is far worse than the person who was just going to borrow the hen."

"Hmm," Lou said.

Jack didn't know what she meant. She looked angry.

"Did you steal the mayor's hen?"

"Borrowed," Jack said.

"Stealing is wrong!" Lou said.

"But if you're going to give something back, it's not stealing."

"It *is* stealing!"

"If you borrow a pen from your mom, then you haven't stolen it, have you?"

"No," Lou said. "But a hen?"

"I just wanted to borrow her so I could find her again."

"I think it's stealing if it's something big."

"A bike is bigger than a hen," Jack said. "If you borrowed my bike and then gave it back, I wouldn't call you a thief."

"No," Lou said. "But ... but ... we're friends."

She shook her head.

"It's giving me a stomachache," she said. "So, it can't be good."

"But the thief is still a lot worse."

Lou was quiet for a long time.

"Yes," she said in the end. "We have to find the thief first, since he's worse."

They called Rusty and asked him to meet them at Jack's granny's house. Lou brought her magnifying glass. Together, she and Jack walked up the hill, past the mayor's farm. The dog was out in the yard and glared at them. Then, it started to bark. Jack tried to hide behind Lou.

"Maybe it was the mayor who took the hen back?" Lou said. "Then there wouldn't be any thieves involved."

"I hope not," Jack said. "Because then all of this would have been for nothing."

The door to the shed was still wide open. Jack hovered behind Lou as she examined every inch around the shed with her magnifying glass. Rusty ran up the hill to them.

"Why did I have to hurry?" Rusty asked.

"We're investigating a break-in," Lou said.

"Why are there so many feathers everywhere?" Rusty wondered.

"You'll have to ask Jack about that," Lou said.

But Jack was so busy looking for clues that he didn't have time to answer.

"We're looking for leads," Lou said.

"When my grandfather was a spy," Jack said, "he found a lead several miles long."

"Not the leash kind of lead," Lou said. "It's a clue, like a footprint or a small object that might help us find the culprit."

"I knew that," Jack snapped.

Lou continued her examination with the magnifying glass. Rusty found a sort of shoelace in the grass.

"I guess this isn't the kind of lead we want," he said, throwing the lace back on the ground.

Lou looked up. "What did you find?"

"Nothing. Just an old shoelace or something like that."

"Let me see," Lou said, picking up the shoelace. "This could be an important clue."

"But why are there so many feathers?" Rusty asked again. "Did the thief have wings?"

"I borrowed the mayor's hen," Jack said. "And now, it's been stolen."

Lou had studied the shoelace long enough.

"If we find the person who's lost this shoelace, then we've found the thief," she said.

"I read about the hen in the paper," Rusty said. "But it didn't say that the mayor had lent it to anyone."

"No ..." Jack said. "He doesn't actually know that I borrowed his hen, so now we have to find it before anyone thinks I'm the thief."

"He didn't know that you borrowed his hen?" Rusty said.

"We have to find the thief super fast, or we're in trouble!" Jack said.

Lou straightened up and put the magnifying glass in her jacket pocket.

"Jack," she said. "*We* are not in trouble! You're the one who stole the mayor's hen. Not Rusty and me. We can help you find the hen. But you'll have to sort out the rest yourself!"

"I'm not a thief," Jack said. "I only borrowed her."

"How can we find out who's missing a shoelace?" Rusty said.

"We'll have to study the shoes of everyone we meet," Lou said. "We have to think of a place where everyone goes."

The shop wasn't open yet, so Jack, Rusty, and Lou
sat on the bench outside and waited. Since no one was
around, there were no shoes to study. The first person
to appear was the shopkeeper, who drove up in his
yellow van. He parked and jumped out. The hood of
his hoodie hung around his face, and the keys on his
keyring jangled as he sauntered toward them.

"Good morning, kids," he said. "You're up and about early."

"We're on a mission," Rusty said.

"Ah," the shopkeeper said. "And what kind of mission is that?"

"We have to find out who took the—" Rusty started, but Lou managed to stop him.

"The bus to the health center," Lou said. "Who took the bus to health center! Or who's going to take it today. How many people."

"We've been asked by the town council's director of buses," Jack said.

"The town council's director of buses?" the shopkeeper echoed. "I've never heard of him."

"My mom works for the council," Lou said. "That's why he asked us."

"I see," said the shopkeeper. "There are a lot of things about the council that I don't know. Anyway, I have to open up."

He went over to the door and searched his keyring for the right key.

"Great, we'll just sit here and count," Lou said.

"That's fine," the shopkeeper said.

He opened the door to the shop and went in. But not long after, he stuck his head out again.

"But ... um ... there's no bus to the health center from here."

"Oh," Lou said. "I forgot. We'll ask the director of buses when we see him."

The shopkeeper muttered something about kids being weird these days and disappeared into the shop again.

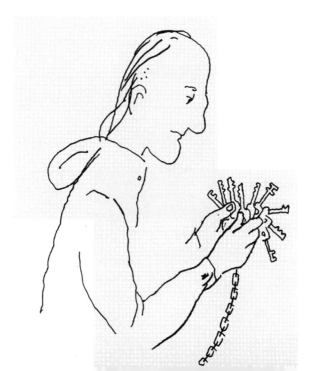

Lou whispered to the others, "We can't let anyone know that we're looking for the hen thief."

"But the shopkeeper's hardly a suspect," Jack said. "He's too nice to be a hen thief."

"You never know," Lou said. "That's the first rule of being a spy."

"Well, anyway, both his shoes had laces," Rusty said.

"My dad's car was stolen once," Jack said. "It was the nicest man in town who took it. Nice people can be really bad."

"He wasn't very nice if he stole the car," Rusty said.

"Let's stick to the facts," Lou said. "We're looking for a hen thief, and we have a shoelace. Until we know more, anyone could be a hen thief. Even if they're nice."

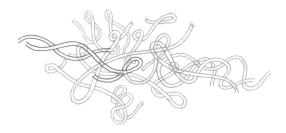

The hours passed, cars parked, and men and women went in and out of the shop. Children went by on bikes, and many others passed by, too. The shoelaces were white, brown, red, black, purple, and more, and everyone had two shoelaces. A black car with dark windows pulled up to the curb.

"Watch out," Rusty said. "It's the car from the bakery."

A woman got out of the car and minced into the shop on high heels.

"No shoelaces there," Lou said.

One of the car windows slid down, and Jack saw Sandy. He leapt up from the bench and went over to her. She barely looked up.

"Nice car," Jack said.

"Whatever," Sandy replied.

"When my dad's famous, we're going to get three new cars."

Sandy yawned.

"My mom actually has hundreds of cars in the United States, and it's a real pain to decide which one to use."

"It's great that you haven't moved yet," Jack said.

"Well, we're thinking about it," Sandy said.

She looked over at Lou and Rusty on the bench.

"Are those your stupid spy friends?"

"We're not spies," Jack said. "We're investigating a break-in. We're actually helping the police."

"My mom has helped the police in the United States with lots of cases, but they're a secret, so I can't say any more."

Sandy's mom came clacking out in her high heels. She smiled at Jack.

"Have you found a friend, Merete?" she said to Sandy as she got in.

Sandy pulled a face.

"Don't, Mom," she said, pressing a button to close the window.

Jack stood and watched the car disappear. When it had pulled out onto the main road, he went back to Lou and Rusty.

"Was that Sandy?" Rusty asked.

"She didn't seem very nice," Lou said.

"Her mom is super famous," Jack said.

"I thought she looked pretty ordinary," Rusty said.

"Well, she isn't," Jack said. "It's fantastic that they've come to live here."

"Can we concentrate on the spying, please?" Lou said.

The sun streamed down on the shop. Four seagulls flew in great circles in the sky above it. A few more hours passed, people came and went, but no one was missing a shoelace. They had been sitting there nearly all day. Lou went home to get them some food. Jack had persuaded his dad to buy them each a bottle of soda. But by now, they'd eaten the food, and the empty bottles were under the bench. Little birds darted around, picking up crumbs.

"Well, a fat lot of good that did us," Jack said. "Look, the shop's closing."

The shopkeeper had opened the door to the shop and put a big cardboard box down on the ground while he got out his keys.

"Are you three still sitting here?" he said. "How many people have taken the mystery bus to the health center today?"

He locked the shop door, pulled up his hood, and picked up the box. It was filled with bags of oats, with some ears of corn lining the sides.

"Maybe a hundred," Rusty said.

"Haha, really?" the shopkeeper laughed.

He carried the box over to the van, opened the back door, and pushed it in.

"It was actually ninety-eight," Jack said. "There was a whole crowd from the church."

"Oh, right, is that so?" the shopkeeper said. "The director of buses will be happy then."

Lou said nothing. She just sat there staring at the shopkeeper's hoodie. He waved to them, then got into the yellow van. The engine coughed and started, and black exhaust belched out.

"Bye for now," the shopkeeper called as he closed the door and drove off, the wheels spitting gravel.

Dust and leaves swirled up, then the exhaust drifted off and the leaves floated down, along with a white feather.

Lou jumped up. The feather landed in her hands. She pulled out her magnifying glass and studied it carefully.

"What do hens eat?" she asked.

"I don't know," Rusty said.

"Sunflower seeds, I think," Jack said. "And lots of other things probably, fruit and seeds and grains."

"Oats?" Lou asked.

The three of them looked at each other. Lou held out the feather. It was just like all the feathers that had been lying around the shed.

"And did you notice the shopkeeper's hoodie?" Lou asked.

The two others looked at each other and shrugged.

"His hoodie was missing the drawstring," Lou said.

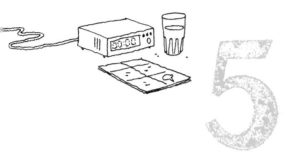

The clock on Jack's bedside table showed four zeros. It was midnight. Black's costume was under the bed, as always, in the blue bag. The house was quiet. Jack took the bag and crept down the ladder, then down the stairs, and out into the dark autumn night. Most of the houses were dark, with only the occasional light still on. He went over to the garage and snuck in. When the door opened again, Black came out. He slipped into the night like a shadow, his cape flying behind him as he ran.

The shopkeeper lived in a small, red house by the river. The superheroes had arranged to meet by the boathouse. Black stood in the shadows behind the boathouse and kept an eye on the road. From there, he could see up the hill he had come down, and he could see the shopkeeper's house on the other side of the field.

He heard footsteps running down the hill.

"Psst," Black whispered. "Over here!"

A blue mask appeared.

"Blue at your service," she whispered, out of breath.

"Black here," Black said.

They sat down by the door to the boathouse and waited for Brown. A half-moon illuminated the clouds as they moved across the sky. There was a cold wind blowing, and Black pulled his cloak tighter around him. They heard footsteps. Someone running. A shadow flitted towards them. It was Brown.

They crept along the side of the road towards the shopkeeper's house. There was a light in the small window by the door, but all the other windows were dark. When they got to the front yard, they ducked down behind the van.

"Do you think the shopkeeper is asleep?" Brown asked. "Do you think it's safe?"

"He's bound to have the hen in the outhouse," Blue said.

There was a huge roll of chicken wire in the long grass by the outhouse.

"Look," Black said. "He's planning to steal more hens."

They tiptoed over to the outhouse. Bending down and without a sound, they snuck around the back. Black got a cobweb over his face; he shuddered and swiftly brushed it off. They peered through the cracks between the planks and tried to see what was inside.

"Let's try to loosen a plank," Black said. "Then we can slip in."

He started to pull at a plank. There was a big, long nail that creaked and groaned, but eventually gave way.

"Be quiet," Blue said. "You'll wake the shopkeeper."

"That was super easy," Black said. He started to pull at the end of another plank. This one was more stubborn, so Brown gave him a hand. They pushed and pulled. Black could feel splinters from the plank in the palm of his hand, but they didn't give up. Slowly, slowly, they worked the nail loose. There was a loud cracking sound, and the outhouse shook. A tile started to slide down the roof towards them.

"Ow!" Blue cried.

The tile had hit her foot.

"Shhh," Black whispered.

Inside, the hen began to cluck.

"Listen," Brown said. "There's a hen in there."

"I think I need to go to the doctor," Blue said. "I might have a broken toe!"

"But we have to catch the hen first," Black said.

"But my toe!" Blue wailed.

"We can't stop now!" Black said.

"I can see the hen," Brown said. He shone his flashlight through the gap they had created. "She's standing in one of the corners."

"We have to abort the mission," Blue said. "It hurts too much."

"Just three more seconds," Black said.

Then, they heard the door to the shopkeeper's house slam.

"Hello?" he shouted.

"Turn off your flashlight," Blue whispered.

"It's not mine," Brown said.

A beam of light swept across the yard, lit up the long grass, and burst through the cracks between the planks of the outhouse.

"Is anyone there?" the shopkeeper shouted.

Blue clapped her hand in front of her mouth. Black looked at her and saw that she had tears in her eyes. They heard the shopkeeper's footsteps coming closer, and the beam from his flashlight continued to sweep from left to right to left. They heard him open the door to the outhouse.

"Did the foxes sniff you out?" they heard the shopkeeper say to the hen. "I'll have to take you indoors for the night."

The hen clucked as he lifted her up. Then, they heard him cross back over to the house. Blue dropped her hand from her mouth.

"We'll have to abort the mission," Brown said. "This is hopeless."

The lights were on inside the house now, and they could see the shopkeeper. He was pacing back and forth.

"We have to find a way to lure the hen out of the house," Black said.

"This is impossible," Blue said. "I have to go home. I might even have to go to the hospital."

Blue couldn't walk on her own and had to hold on to the two other superheroes as she hobbled towards the road. They eventually made it back to the boathouse and up the dark slope.

Jack had rung Lou's doorbell at least ten times, but no one had come to the door. So he left and went up the road to Rusty's house. Rusty was home, and they went back to Lou's together, but there was still no answer. They sat down on the steps to wait. Jack wanted to leave after a while and had just started to crawl through the hedge when they heard a car turn onto the driveway.

"Hi Rusty," Lou's mom called and waved.

Jack crawled back out of the hedge. Lou was in the car, and her mother helped her out. She had a cast on her foot and needed crutches to walk.

"Oh," Jack said. "Was it that bad?"

Lou's mother looked at Jack and Rusty.

"Did you know that Lou had hurt herself last night?" she asked.

"Um … no," Jack said. "But it looks bad; that's all I meant."

"I managed to hurt my foot last night," Lou said. "I tripped, and an old vase fell on it."

"That old vase really shouldn't have been standing in the hall," her mom said.

"It's a shame about the vase," Lou said.

"So, a vase fell on your foot?" Rusty repeated.

"Yes, and I've broken one of the bones. The doctor said it was a very complicated break."

"It was just one of my mother's old vases," Lou's mom said.

"Yeah, and luckily, it wasn't a very nice one," Lou added. "My dad was always saying that he wished it would fall and smash into a thousand pieces."

Rusty and Jack laughed.

"Well, lucky it was that one that fell on your foot then," Jack said.

Lou hobbled up the stairs to her room. Jack and Rusty followed, closing the door so her mom wouldn't hear them.

"The doctor couldn't believe that it was just a vase," Lou said. "But I told him it was a very heavy old vase, and in the end, he believed me."

"How are we going to get the hen now?" Jack asked.

"We'll have to give up," Lou said. "Maybe we should call the police and let them sort it out."

"I agree," Rusty said. "Then they can arrest the shopkeeper."

"We can't call the police," Jack said.

"Well, there's certainly nothing I can do," Lou said.

"Yes there is," Jack said. "You can spy on the shopkeeper when Rusty and I go back to get the hen."

"Yeah, you can sit by the shop and keep an eye on him," Rusty said.

"You want me just to sit there?" Lou said.

"You're so good at spying," Rusty said. "You can pretend to sell waffles for the school fundraiser."

"But I'm not even on any of the school teams," Lou said. "I think we should call the police."

"You can sell waffles to raise money for children in poor countries," Rusty said.

"Good idea," Jack chimed in.

"I don't know," Lou said. "It might work, but we have to be careful; I think the shopkeeper suspects us already."

They sat together and planned for hours. Lou would take care of the waffle batter. They would all start out

138

together at the shop. Then Black and Brown would head back to the shopkeeper's house. They would stay in touch via walkie-talkie. Lou insisted that they use secret codes so nobody else would know what they were talking about. "The waffles are cold" meant there was no danger, and "the waffles are warm" meant that the shopkeeper was on his way. When Jack got home, he went down to the cellar again. He struggled to get

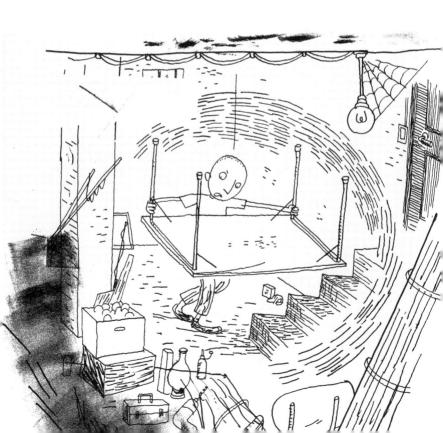

out an old camping table. It was covered with brown, sticky stains. He managed to haul it up the stairs, just as his mother appeared.

"Why have you dragged out that old table?" she asked.

"Lou's going to borrow it," Jack said.

He went into the kitchen to get a rag and started to wash it down.

"You should wash it properly," his mother said. "What are you up to now?"

"I need to borrow the waffle iron as well," Jack said. "Lou's going to raise money for children in poor countries."

"That's kind of her," his mother said. "Go and get a bucket of warm water and some detergent."

Jack's dad helped him carry the table and the waffle iron to the shop. Rusty and Lou were already there. Lou sat on the bench with her crutches beside her, as well as a big bowl of waffle batter and a poster.

"We need electricity," Lou said. "We're going to have to ask the shopkeeper."

"Is that a good idea?" Rusty asked. "He might get suspicious."

But before they had time to think, the shopkeeper came out. Jack noticed the missing drawstring on his hoodie. The shopkeeper nodded at them, then noticed the camping table and waffle iron.

"What are you up to?" he asked.

"Oh no, we've been caught," Lou whispered.

"We were going to ask you nicely if we could use

Support
children
in Swed

Poor

en

10 kr.

one of your sockets," Rusty said. "We really want to help poor children."

"Hmm," said the shopkeeper, coming closer. He saw the poster.

"Support poor children in Sweden," he read out loud. "That's the most ridiculous thing I've ever heard. There aren't any poor children in Sweden."

"I actually knew that," Jack said. "They are much poorer in other countries."

"Well, then we'd better change the poster," Lou said.

"Come on," the shopkeeper said. "I'll show you where there's a socket, and I've got an extension cord you can use. And a marker, so you can change your silly poster."

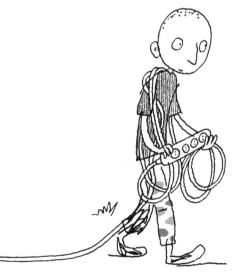

He guffawed as he walked back to the door.

"Phew," Rusty whispered. "He doesn't seem to suspect us."

"Shhh," Lou said. "Act normal!"

Lou sat on the bench and waited while Jack and Rusty went into the shop with the shopkeeper. They came back with the extension cord and marker. Then they crossed out "Sweden" and wrote "poor countries," instead. Not long after, the smell of waffles started to waft around the shop entrance and up the street.

Jack and Rusty took off, leaving Lou to deal with the waffles and keep an eye on the shopkeeper. When Jack and Rusty got to the boathouse, near where the shopkeeper lived, Jack turned on the walkie-talkie. At the start, there was a low wailing noise and then lots of crackling.

"Hello, hello," Jack said. "How are the waffles? Over."

They heard Lou's voice through all the beeps and crackles.

"The waffles are cold," she said. "I repeat: The waffles are cold. Over."

"Received, over and out," Jack said.

He looked at Rusty and nodded.

They had hidden two bags under the boathouse, from which they produced their costumes. They covered their faces with their masks and tied their capes at their necks. They moved stealthily, like two shadows, along the forest's edge. It wasn't dark, so they had to be extra careful. They bent down low and ran through the cornfield. Soon they were at the house. Black looked in through one of the windows. It was dark inside. They walked around the house and tested the front door. It was locked. Brown ran over to the outhouse, and the door was wide open, but there was no hen in sight. They went around the back of the house. Tall grass grew up against the wall. Then, they spotted a trapdoor to the cellar. It creaked when they pulled it open. Beetles scuttled away from the light. It smelled like a sewer.

"We'll have to go down there," Brown said. "It might be the only way in."

"I don't think there are any hens down there in the dark," Black said. "And it smells like an old toilet."

"Would your grandfather have let the smell of a toilet stop him?" Brown said.

Brown went down the stairs first and came to another door. It was fastened with a hook. He flicked it open. Black was still at the top watching him.

"Come on," Brown said. "Are we going to get this hen or not?"

"Ye–es …"

Black followed Brown into the pitch-black cellar. The stench made him retch. It was impossible to see where they were. There was a clatter, and Brown groaned.

"Ow," he said. "We'll have to watch out."

"That's impossible," Black said.

"We have to find the stairs," Brown said.

They fumbled their way forward through wet cobwebs. Black stuck close to Brown. Eventually, their eyes adjusted to the dark. They could see wooden trunks, styrofoam boxes, and dusty, old advertisements.

"This way," Brown whispered. "I can see the stairs."

They clambered over a pile of green fruit boxes to get to the bottom of the narrow staircase. Each step creaked as they went up. The door at the top was open, and they emerged into the light of the shopkeeper's hallway.

"It won't take long to find the hen now," Black said. He ran from room to room.

"Here, *chick chick chick*," he called.

Brown went upstairs. Black could hear him running through the rooms.

"*Chick chick chick*, where are you?" Black called.

The living room was full of white feathers, and in the corner behind the TV, the shopkeeper had closed off a small area with chicken wire.

And there was the mayor's prizewinning hen.

"Found her!" Black shouted to Brown. He looked at her and said in a soothing voice, "I've come to rescue you from the evil shopkeeper."

He looked around.

"I just need to find something to carry you in, because we forgot to take a sack, and we should have brought one ..."

Brown came into the room.

"Good work," he said.

The walkie-talkie crackled to life. They could only just hear Lou's voice.

Black took off his cape and promptly threw it over the hen, then swung it up over his shoulder.

"We're going to liberate you now," Black whispered.

They heard the sound of a car approaching. And they saw the shopkeeper's van on the other side of the field. A dust cloud trailed behind it. It was coming towards them at full speed. Brown and Black were paralyzed with fright as they saw the van whiz past the window.

They heard a door slam. Suddenly, Brown came to life.

"Run down to the cellar!" he shouted.

The two superheroes slipped through the cellar door and only just managed to close it before the shopkeeper entered through the front door. He walked down the hall, past the cellar door, and then they heard him rummaging around, his voice coaxing the hen.

"Come on, my prizewinning beauty! You can come out now!"

Black and Brown started down the stairs as carefully as they could, but the steps still creaked. They stopped. Black could feel his heart racing. The shopkeeper had also fallen silent.

"It's a good thing we've got our superhero costumes on," Brown said. "If he sees us, he won't know who we are."

Then, they heard the shopkeeper's voice again.

"Come on, Plucky-Clucky, here's some corn!"

Black and Brown continued to creep down the stairs, which creaked each step of the way. When they reached the bottom, the walkie-talkie beeped loudly.

The door at the top of the stairs was wrenched open. The boys were almost blinded by the light.

"Run!" Brown shouted, and the two boys stumbled over and through the empty boxes.

"Hey! Stop!" the shopkeeper shouted after them.

Black and Brown were soon outside again, and they slammed the trapdoor shut.

"Run back to the boathouse," Brown shouted.

Black looked at the boathouse at the other end of the field. The field seemed endless.

"We'll never make it," Black said.

COME BACK, YOU ROGUES!

He dashed off around the side of the house. Brown hurtled after him. They ran past the parked van.

"We can hide in the outhouse," he whispered.

They could hear the shopkeeper roaring on the other side of the house.

They ran to the door of outhouse. But when Black tried to open it, he saw it was locked.

"A padlock!" he shouted. "What do we do now?"

"I'm not going to harm you!" the shopkeeper shouted behind them.

"Quick!" Black said. "Let's jump in the back of the van."

Without another word, Brown opened the back doors of the van and jumped in. He put out his hand to help Black with the bundle. They pulled the door shut and cowered behind some empty cardboard boxes. It smelled of rotten bananas, and they couldn't see a thing. They heard the shopkeeper shouting to them outside, asking them to come out.

"Nothing will happen to you, just give me back the hen!" he shouted.

"No one's allowed to beat children," Brown whispered.

"Just let him try," Black whispered back. "My uncle's actually a policeman, and I can call him anytime."

The walkie-talkie beeped again. Brown tried to wrap it in his cape to muffle the sound.

"Lou here!" they heard a voice say through all the crackling. "Do you need any more eggs for the waffles? I repeat: Do you need any more eggs? Over."

"We have to answer," Brown whispered.

"We have to be quiet," Black whispered. "If he finds us now, he'll lock us up with the hen."

"I'm going to answer," Brown whispered.

He pressed the button and spoke as quietly as he could into the microphone. "The batter is ready, but we can't get out. Over."

"I can't hear you," Lou shouted.

There was more beeping and crackling. They couldn't hear the shopkeeper anymore.

"We're trapped in the back of the shopkeeper's van," Brown said, a little louder. "Back of the van! Over!"

As soon as he'd said that, the doors opened. The light streamed in, and the cardboard boxes they

158

had hidden behind were far too small to hide two boys. The shopkeeper stood there glaring at them. His face was red, and his eyes were flashing. Black tried to creep even further back, but there was nowhere to go. The shopkeeper pointed at the bundle in Black's hands.

"Give me that!" he demanded. "I knew that you were after something …"

Black held on to the bundle.

"Why do you have those silly masks on?" the shopkeeper said. "Give me the hen, now!"

Brown pulled off his mask and became Rusty again.

"Give him the hen," he whispered. "Then we might get out of here alive."

"Give me the hen, now!" the shopkeeper roared. "You won't get away!"

"It's not your hen," Black said.

"Of course it's mine," the shopkeeper laughed.

"You've stolen it," Black said.

"Absolutely not," the shopkeeper said. "Give me the hen, now. It's mine!"

159

"We're done for," Rusty whispered. "We just have to give him the hen."

Now Black pulled off his mask, and became Jack.

"You stole the hen," Jack said. "From the mayor!"

"Nah! I saved it," the shopkeeper sneered. "It was stuck in that tiny shed for days. It could have died."

"That's my granny's shed. I found the hen in the forest and managed to lure it into the shed. I was going to tell the mayor."

"I don't believe you," the shopkeeper said. "It was clucking and making noise for days before I eventually broke in. I saved it."

"I was sick," Jack said.

"He actually was sick," Rusty confirmed.

"So, there you go," Jack said. "And by the time I was better again, you'd stolen the hen."

"I'm sure the mayor would love to hear that you've stolen his hen," Rusty said to the shopkeeper.

"She's so beautiful," the shopkeeper said. "I had to save her, no matter what. I haven't stolen … I …"

Suddenly, the shopkeeper became aggressive again.

"Nah," he said. "The mayor will never believe a couple of kids. Give me the hen! Now!"

"Never," Jack said. "I'm going straight to the mayor."

"Okay, tell him I'm the hen thief then. Go on, why don't you? He'll never believe you! No one listens to silly children!"

Jack looked around, terrified. There was nothing that could save them now. No doors, nothing to hide behind. Rusty was clutching the walkie-talkie beside him. He looked at Jack, eyes wide with fear.

"We have to surrender," he whispered.

Jack looked at the walkie-talkie again. Then, he looked at the shopkeeper. He was really angry now, but Jack grabbed the walkie-talkie and sat up. He held the bundle tight under his arm.

"He will," Jack said. "Because we've recorded everything you've said."

He held up the walkie-talkie.

"You have to let us go immediately, or Lou will take this recording to the mayor."

"Huh?" the shopkeeper said.

His mouth fell open, and he stared at the walkie-talkie. Rusty looked up at Jack, astonished, but was quick to scramble to his feet.

"Yes, exactly," Rusty said. "Everything's been recorded. You'll go to jail if you don't let us go immediately!"

"But …" the shopkeeper stammered. "I haven't said …"

"You've said enough. Let's see who the mayor and the police believe now."

"Yes," Rusty said. "And Jack's uncle is actually a policeman, so you'll be in trouble if you don't let us go."

"Exactly," Jack said. "Well, nearly one."

The shopkeeper stepped back and looked down at the ground.

"Fine, scram!" he said. "And take that stupid hen with you! She doesn't even lay eggs!"

Jack and Rusty jumped out of the van. The shopkeeper glared at them.

"You'd better run now," he shouted, "before I change my mind and give you a beating!"

"Beating children is illegal," Rusty said, before he and Jack shot off.

When Lou's mother opened the door, Jack and Rusty were so out of breath that they couldn't say a word. They just stood there gasping, their faces bright red. Lou's mother gave them a funny look. Jack tried to hide the bundle with the hen behind his back.

"Lou's in her room," her mother said, letting them in.

Lou was sitting at her desk, counting the money she'd made selling waffles. She listened to what her

friends had to say. The hen wandered around the room, clucking, and eventually settled into a corner behind the bed.

"And then, Jack lied and said we had a recording, and that made the shopkeeper think again." Rusty laughed. "You should have seen his face."

They laughed together.

"It's a good thing you're so good at lying," Rusty said.

"Me?" Jack said.

"Yes, you're so funny when you say all that stuff," Lou giggled.

"I never lie," Jack said.

Lou and Rusty looked at each other and burst out laughing all over again.

"I don't," Jack said. "Anyway, we have to call the newspaper so I can give the hen back."

"I've got the number of a reporter," Lou said, pulling a piece of paper out from the money box.

"Where did you get that?" Jack asked.

"I spoke to him when I was selling waffles," Lou

said. "He was so impressed that I wanted to help poor children that he interviewed me."

"Are you going to be in the paper?" Jack said.

"Wow!" Rusty exclaimed.

"It'll probably only be a small column," Jack said.

"Where's the hen?" Lou said.

"She's right here," Rusty said.

She had stopped clucking and was sitting on a cushion at the back of Lou's bed.

"Maybe we should get her out of here before my mom notices," Lou said.

"Come and look!" Rusty exclaimed. "She's laid an egg!"

The trees were waving their yellow leaves, and sunlight was glinting off the puddles on the road. A seagull was sitting high up on the church spire, waiting for something to happen. Down in a field, four brown horses were grazing. Suddenly, a small red car, which had been driving along the road past the houses, swung into the yard outside the mayor's house. A plump man with lots of curly hair jumped out of the car. He had a camera around his neck and a notepad in his breast pocket. The mayor's dog started to bark immediately. The mayor came out onto the steps. He knew the man who had come to visit.

"What do you want to interview me about now?" he said to the newspaper reporter.

The reporter pulled out his notepad.

"How does it feel to have your prizewinning hen back?"

The mayor gave him a baffled look. He scanned the henhouse where the prizewinning hen liked to strut around, but she wasn't there.

"What are you talking about?"

"Your prizewinning hen!" the journalist said. "I got a phone call saying that she had finally been returned."

"Someone is messing with you, then," the mayor said. "Liars!"

"Excuse me?"

The reporter seemed to be shocked. "Lying to the newspaper," he said. "That's outrageous! Why would anyone—"

"But if I ever do find out who the thief is, I'll call you straightaway," the mayor said. "That crook deserves to have his name and photo in the paper, so everyone knows what kind of …"

The mayor balled his fists as he spoke.

"Well, well, well, I'd better be off again, then," the reporter said.

He got back into his car and was about to turn the key in the ignition when he spotted a small procession.

At the front came Jack, wearing a backpack. Rusty was beside him. And behind them were other local boys and girls. Jack had told them he was going to be in the newspaper, so they'd followed along on their bikes to see.

"What's this?" the mayor wondered.

The reporter jumped out of the car again, and they both stood and watched the procession approach. The reporter lifted his camera and took a couple of pictures.

"I've come to return your prizewinning hen!" Jack said.

The children stopped in front of the mayor, and Jack took off his backpack. He held it out to the mayor.

"I saved her from the wolves and foxes in the forest," Jack said.

"You've found my hen!" the mayor exclaimed. He opened the backpack, and the hen looked up at him. The mayor had tears in his eyes.

"Thank you! Thank you all!" he said.

"No, it was just me who ..." Jack started to say.

"What a great story!" the reporter said. "Tell me more about the wolves."

"Well, I was walking in the forest on my own when I heard this noise ..."

"Fantastic!" the mayor said. He held the hen in his arms and kissed her head. "So, she got lost, and you found her!"

"Tell me more," the reporter said. "How did you manage to chase off the wolves?"

"But ... But ..." Jack said. "I was the one who heard the hen clucking, and I'd read in the paper that the mayor..."

"Incredible!" the reporter said. "We've never heard of any wolves in the forest before, so this will definitely be front-page news."

"Really?" Jack said.

"Oh, my fantastic hen!" the mayor cried with joy. "How can I thank you enough?"

"It was only me ..." Jack tried to say. "The wolf was really scary, and I threw sticks at it. The hen was petrified."

"I have to say, the children in this municipality are really something," the mayor said. "They deserve a reward!"

"But, but … I was the one who …" Jack tried again to be heard.

"You could give us a soccer field!" one of the girls shouted.

"Yes!" several of the children cheered.

"Let me get a picture of you and the hen," the reporter said to the mayor.

"A soccer field?" the mayor said in surprise.

"The town council could build us a new soccer field," the girl shouted again. "Aren't you the head of the council?"

"Yes, yes, I am …" the mayor started.

"Keep still a second so I can take a photograph," the reporter said.

"Aren't I going to be in the photograph?" Jack said.

"Yes, of course," the reporter replied. "You stand there!"

He pointed and fiddled with his camera lens.

"What about us?" one of the boys in the group said.

"Yes, of course, you too!" shouted the reporter. "All of you, go and stand behind the mayor!"

176

"But I was the one who actually found the hen!" Jack protested.

The whole group moved and stood together behind Jack and the mayor. Rusty stood next to Jack.

"And Rusty helped me," Jack said.

"You kids are amazing," the reporter said.

Everyone was talking at the same time, and the hen, who had begun to cluck, turned her head and cautiously flapped her wings.

"I was the one who…" Jack tried again.

The reporter looked at him for a moment.

"You can hold the hen!" he said. "That'll make a good picture."

The mayor gave the hen to Jack.

"Be careful," he said. "She's getting nervous with all the noise."

The hen clucked and twisted in his arms.

"Quiet now!" the reporter shouted. "And smile!"

Just as the reporter took the picture, the prizewinning hen flew up, and there were feathers everywhere.

"She's frightened," the mayor said, chasing after the hen as she ran around the yard.

"Man, it's going to be a great newspaper tomorrow," the reporter said before hopping back into his little red car. A cloud of dust rose up as the car raced off down the hill.

"He was in a hurry," Rusty said.

"I'm going to be on the front page!" Jack said.

The mayor was stroking the hen, his eyes full of tears.

Jack walked home and jumped over all the slugs on the road. He saw the car with the dark windows from the bakery parked outside the shop. Jack didn't want to run into the shopkeeper, but he still snuck over to the car to look through the windows. They were so dark it was impossible to see anything. But as he stood there staring, he heard a voice behind him.

"Are you ever going to stop spying on me?"

It was Sandy.

"I just wanted to tell you something," Jack said.

"It's really annoying to have you spying on me all the time," Sandy said.

"You can stay here now," Jack said.

"Oh?" Sandy said. "What if we don't want to?"

"Well, I'm famous now, too!"

"You?" Sandy said with a snort.

"Yes, there's going to be a photograph of me on the front page of tomorrow's newspaper," Jack said.

"Nah, that's nothing," Sandy said. "My mom's in the paper every day in the United States."

"Every day?" Jack said. "How does she manage that?"

"It's easy when you're as famous as she is," Sandy said.

Her mother came out of the shop. She smiled at the shopkeeper, who had appeared in the doorway. When he saw Jack, he pulled a face. Jack tried to hide behind Sandy.

"Thank you. Such excellent service," Sandy's mother said to the shopkeeper with a grin.

"We've moved to a marvelous place, Merete!" she continued. "I think we're going to be very happy here."

Sandy didn't answer. She got back into the car and closed the door. Her mother carried on chatting with the shopkeeper. Jack slipped away quietly.

The next morning, Jack woke up to the smell of coffee.
The sunlight was pouring in through the windows,
and he heard his mother singing in the kitchen. He was
about to turn over and wrap himself up in his quilt
again when he suddenly remembered: the newspaper!
He leapt out of bed. He couldn't get his pants on fast
enough and tried to put on a T-shirt as he climbed
down the ladder. He lost his footing on the bottom
rung but landed on his feet. He ran barefoot across

the gravel to the mailbox. It was always full of pincher bugs. Jack had to shake the paper well before taking it inside. The earwigs fell to the ground and scurried off. He opened the newspaper. On the front page, it said in bold letters: "WOLVES IN THE FOREST." There were no photographs of Jack, or the hen, or the mayor, but under the headline it read: "Mayor's prizewinning hen saved from hungry wolf pack. Read more on pages 4 and 5."

"But that's not what I said," Jack muttered to himself.

His mother was now sitting at the table and had to move the cheese and milk carton when Jack spread the newspaper out on the table.

"What are you reading?" his mom asked.

Jack didn't answer, but quickly turned to pages 4 and 5.

"Oh, look, there's Rusty!" his mother exclaimed.

In the photograph, the hen was flapping its wings, and there were feathers flying everywhere. The mayor was standing beside the hen with a big smile, and behind the mayor were the faces of all the other children. Rusty appeared on the side of the photograph.

"But I'm not there," Jack said.

"These brave children chased away the pack of wolves and saved the mayor's hen," read the caption.

"But that's not true!" Jack burst out. "That's total garbage!"

"Never believe what you read in the papers," his mom said. "They always lie!"

"But I'm not even in the picture!" Jack said.

He had tears in his eyes.

"But it's fun that Rusty's there," his mom said.

Jack pushed the newspaper away and slumped down in his chair. His mother poured a cup of coffee and started to leaf through the paper.

"Now I'll never be famous!" Jack wailed.

"Oh, look," his mother exclaimed again, "there's Lou!"

Jack looked over at the newspaper. There was a big picture of Lou selling waffles outside the shop. "Lou's waffles raise money to help starving children," the caption read.

"You've got some famous friends," his mother said, laughing.

Jack stood up abruptly and hurried out of the kitchen. He shoved his feet into his sneakers and left the house. He could hear his dad playing guitar in the garage. Jack went out onto the road. There was a large crow sitting on a lamppost. It stared straight down at him. Jack stuck out his tongue. He wondered if he should go see Lou, but he couldn't face her. Then he thought maybe he'd go to Rusty's instead and

started to walk there, but he turned back halfway. As he passed the shop, he saw the shopkeeper stacking banana boxes. Jack took a detour to avoid being seen. He crept along, hiding behind the trees and cans on the other side of the road. He had almost made it to his destination when the shopkeeper spotted him.

"Oh, it's you," he said.

"Yep, it's me," Jack said.

The shopkeeper continued what he was doing. Jack stood there and glared at him.

"Don't you have anything better to do?" the shopkeeper asked.

"Like what?" Jack said.

"Why are you in such a bad mood?" the shopkeeper asked. "After all, you won. You got the hen."

"I'm not in a bad mood," Jack said. "I'm the one who gave the hen back, but everyone besides me ended up in the newspaper."

"Newspaper?" the shopkeeper said. "Forget it, I wouldn't want to be in that stupid rag."

"But you have to be in the newspaper to be famous."

187

"Being famous isn't the most important thing," the shopkeeper said. "Making lots of money is better!"

"Is it?"

"If I could make just a little bit more money from milk and eggs, I would have a swimming pool in the garden, and maybe I'd buy a new car and a suit, a white suit that I could wear on vacation. In Italy."

"Or China," Jack said.

"Yes!" the shopkeeper exclaimed. "Or China! I'd buy my own jet plane so I could travel wherever I wanted!"

"And you could have a boat, too," Jack said. "As big as a city. So big you could take all your friends with you."

"Yes, an enormous boat," the shopkeeper said. "Ha, that would be just the thing!"

"Yes, fantastic!" Jack said.

The shopkeeper shook his head.

"But for now, I have to work. Standing here dreaming all day won't make me rich. Can you help me with these boxes?"

"You want me to work?"

"Well, you have to work if you want to make money."

"Will I make money?"

"Hmm," the shopkeeper said. "If you help me with these banana boxes, you'll get some ice cream, at least."

"And a soda?" Jack said.

The shopkeeper laughed and dropped a couple of boxes into Jack's arms. They were heavy.

"We'll see," he said, popping another box on top.

Håkon Øvreås is a celebrated poet, with several published collections. *Brown*, his first book for children, has been a runaway success in Norway and has received numerous awards, including the Norwegian Ministry of Culture's Literature Prize. A global bestseller, *Brown* has also been published in at least 32 languages throughout the world, and received the Batchelder Award for the most outstanding children's translation published in the United States in 2014. This book, which is the sequel to *Brown*, and *Blue*, the last book in the trilogy, have been equally successful.

An illustrator and cartoonist, **Øyvind Torseter** is one of Norway's most acclaimed cultural figures. He works in both traditional and digital media and has received great recognition and numerous prizes. His books *My Father's Arms Are a Boat* (Batchelder Honor), *The Hole*, *Why Dogs Have Wet Noses*, *The Heartless Troll*, *Brown* (Batchelder Award), *The Most Beautiful Story* (Batchelder Honor), and *The Bird Coat* are also available in English from Enchanted Lion Books.

Born in Edinburgh, Scotland, **Kari Dickson** grew up bilingually, speaking English in her daily life and Norwegian with her mother and grandparents. She holds a B.A. in Scandinavian studies and an M.A. in translation. She has translated many of the Norwegian books published by Enchanted Lion, including Batchelder Award winner *Brown*, and Batchelder Honor books *My Father's Arms Are a Boat* and *The Most Beautiful Story*.